Agnes
and
Clarabelle

**READ & BLOOM BOOKS**

Agnes
and
Clarabelle

Adele Griffin and Courtney Sheinmel
illustrated by Sara Palacios

BLOOMSBURY
NEW YORK   LONDON   OXFORD   NEW DELHI   SYDNEY

For Aunt Biz —A. G.
For Elana M. & Llen P. —C. S.
For both my grandmothers, Sarita and Elena —S. P.

First published in the United States of America in January 2017
by Bloomsbury Children's Books
www.bloomsbury.com

Bloomsbury is a registered trademark of Bloomsbury Publishing Plc

For information about permission to reproduce selections from this book, write to
Permissions, Bloomsbury Children's Books, 1385 Broadway, New York, New York 10018
Bloomsbury books may be purchased for business or promotional use. For information on bulk purchases
please contact Macmillan Corporate and Premium Sales Department at specialmarkets@macmillan.com

Library of Congress Cataloging-in-Publication Data
Griffin, Adele, author.
Agnes and Clarabelle / by Adele Griffin and Courtney Sheinmel ; illustrated by Sara Palacios.
pages   cm
Summary: Best friends Agnes Pig and Clarabelle Chicken share their favorite activities for each season,
from collecting chestnuts in winter, to celebrating Clarabelle's birthday in spring, to spending a day at the
beach in summer, to buying new sneakers in autumn.
ISBN 978-1-61963-137-3 (hardcover)
ISBN 978-1-61963-969-0 (e-book) • ISBN 978-1-61963-970-6 (e-PDF)
[1. Best friends—Fiction. 2. Friendship—Fiction. 3. Seasons—Fiction. 4. Pigs—Fiction. 5. Chickens—
Fiction.] I. Sheinmel, Courtney, author. II. Palacios, Sara, illustrator. III. Title.
PZ7.G881325Ag 2017   [E]—dc23   2015010336

Art created with colored pencil, watercolor, and digital tools
Typeset in Goudy Oldstyle and Cinderella
Book design by John Candell
Printed in China by C&C Offset Printing Co., Ltd., Shenzhen, Guangdong
1 3 5 7 9 10 8 6 4 2

All papers used by Bloomsbury Publishing, Inc., are natural, recyclable products
made from wood grown in well-managed forests. The manufacturing processes
conform to the environmental regulations of the country of origin.

Contents

Chapter 1
Spring: Surprise Party

"Agnes!" said Clarabelle Chicken. "Do you know what spring means?"

"Spring means the robin family is laying eggs, and spring means there

are always fresh rain puddles to jump in," said Agnes Pig.

"And spring means MY BIRTHDAY!" squawked Clarabelle.

"Yes, that too," said Agnes.

"And do you know what I love even more than my birthday?" asked Clarabelle. "My birthday party!"

"I would like to throw a surprise party for your birthday," said Agnes.

"*Eeeee!*" Clarabelle ruffled her feathers. "Nobody ever threw me a surprise party before! Can I help plan it?"

"Yes," said Agnes. "Let's plan your surprise party together."

"Where should we have it?" asked Clarabelle.

"Anywhere you want," said Agnes.

Clarabelle thought about different places.

The roller rink was too crashy.

The pool was too splashy.

The bowling lanes were too smashy.

"I have an idea!" said Clarabelle. "Why don't you have my surprise party at your house?"

4

"Yes, that's the best place for a party," agreed Agnes.

Agnes and Clarabelle went to the party store.

"Sunshine yellow is my favorite color," said Clarabelle. "Next comes hot pink. Then grape purple. Then cherry red. Then all the ocean colors. But sunshine yellow is my favorite!"

They bought six yellow party hats, six yellow plates and six yellow cups, and one large yellow paper tablecloth. They bought six hot pink balloons because the store was out of yellow.

"Can we play hopscotch at my

party?" asked Clarabelle. "Chickens are excellent hoppers."

"Yes, and we'll also play Lemon on a Spoon," answered Agnes.

"What kind of a game is that?"
asked Clarabelle.

"It is a race to see who can walk
fastest while balancing a lemon

on a spoon," said Agnes. "Pigs are magnificent balancers."

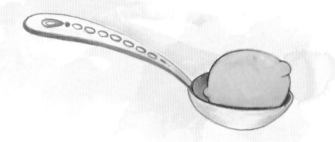

"I think there should be prizes for the winners," Clarabelle said.

"We will get prizes for everyone," Agnes said.

"This party sounds so good," said Clarabelle.

The night before the party,

Clarabelle stayed over at Agnes's house.

But Clarabelle could not sleep.

"What if the invitations got

Shh! It's a
surprise party

for
Clarabelle

stuck in the mailbox slot?" asked Clarabelle.

"I heard them fall down to the bottom," said Agnes.

"All of them?"

"Yes—one each for Jake Rabbit and Thomas Cat and Mallory Duck and Willa Goat."

"Plus you and me. That makes six," said Clarabelle. "But what if Willa forgets to come? She forgets everything."

"She won't forget," said Agnes.

"What if she finds something better to do?"

"Nothing is better than a surprise party for you," Agnes assured her.

"That's true. But what if I am sick tomorrow?" asked Clarabelle.

Agnes got up. She stuck a thermometer in Clarabelle's beak. "You are one healthy chicken," she said.

"What if everyone comes and

nobody has a good time?" asked
Clarabelle.

But Agnes was asleep.

In the morning, Agnes and
Clarabelle set up for the party. Agnes
put the cups and plates on the table.

Clarabelle pecked an ice sculpture for the middle.

Then Clarabelle went back to her house. She stood by her window. She watched Jake and Thomas and Mallory walk into Agnes's house.

From across the street, Agnes twitched her snout. That was the signal to come over.

But where was Willa?

Six plates, six cups, six hats—but five friends? That didn't work!

In the window across the street,
Agnes twitched her snout again
and tapped her watch. It was 12:59.
Clarabelle had to be surprised at one
o'clock.

Clarabelle did not want to be late for her surprise. She hurried across the street to Agnes's house.

She counted to ten.

Then she opened the door.

"Surprise!" Jake and Thomas and Mallory and Agnes called out.

Clarabelle's eyes got shiny. "I'm so happy," she said.

"I guess Willa forgot," Agnes whispered.

"That's okay," Clarabelle said. "Even if my birthday's not perfect, it's still perfect."

Chapter 2
Summer: Beach Day

The sun was shining hot in the bright blue sky.

Agnes shut the curtains. She called Clarabelle on the phone.

"Clarabelle," said Agnes. "Bad

news. My parents have decided to
spend the day at the beach."

"I love the beach!" said Clarabelle.
"And today is the perfect day to go
there!"

"I've never been there before,"
said Agnes. "And I don't like new
places."

"Then I will go with you!" said
Clarabelle. Her tail feathers shook
with excitement. "We can make sand
chickens! And peck for shells! And
race seagulls!"

"It's a long drive," said Agnes.

"That's one of the best parts.
We'll have time to play car games,"
said Clarabelle. "There's Twenty

Questions and I Spy with My Little
Bird Eye!"

But in the car, Agnes could
not play games. She was too busy

thinking about the beach. And the more Agnes thought about the beach, the more she wished she could go back home.

"The first thing I'm going to do is get a birdseed snow cone!" Clarabelle declared. "Then I'm going to boogie board."

"I don't feel so good," Agnes said.

"What's wrong?" asked Clarabelle.

"I have to go to the bathroom."

"Sometimes you feel like you have

to go, but then you don't," Clarabelle reminded her. "I will tell you a joke to distract you. 'Why did the chicken cross the road?'"

"To get away from the beach," answered Agnes.

"We'll do jokes later," Clarabelle said. She squeezed Agnes's hoof.

"I'm sorry that my hoof is so sweaty," Agnes told her.

"I don't mind," Clarabelle replied.

"I have to go to the bathroom

very badly," said Agnes. "Very, VERY
badly."

"More jokes," said Clarabelle.
"Cluck-cluck."

"Who's there?" Agnes asked.

"Omelette!"

"Omelette who?"

"Omelette smarter than I look!"
Clarabelle squawked with laughter.
Agnes smiled.

They got to the gas station, but Agnes did not have to go to the bathroom anymore. "Last joke," Clarabelle said. "Why *didn't* the chicken cross the road?"

"Why?" Agnes asked.

"Because she was already at the beach! Look—I can see the ocean!"

They pulled into the parking lot.

Agnes watched Clarabelle grab her pail and shovel. She watched Clarabelle swing her beach towel over her wing.

Clarabelle opened the door and hopped out. But Agnes didn't move from her seat.

"Come on," Clarabelle said. "What are you waiting for? I spy with my little bird eye the perfect wave! Surf's up!"

"I'm scared of a wave knocking me over or a Frisbee hitting my head." Agnes poked her snout out the window. "And the sky is too big. I can't see the end of it."

Clarabelle looked up at the sky. She tried to see what Agnes saw.

"Everything will be fine once we're out there," said Clarabelle. "You'll love it."

"You go," Agnes told Clarabelle. "You love the beach. But I will feel better in the car."

Clarabelle had an idea. She spread the towel on the parking-lot sand. She flipped open their beach chairs.

"Agnes," she said, "come sit with me. The sun is shining. We can hear the ocean. We can smell the salty air. We can stay right by the car."

Agnes got out of the car. She sat in her beach chair.

"This is very nice," she said. She closed her eyes to enjoy the breeze on her face. Then she opened her

eyes and saw all the other cars in the parking lot. "But we are not really at the beach."

"We are at the beach enough," said Clarabelle. "I spy with my little bird eye—something blue!"

Chapter 3
Fall: New Sneakers

"Look at this, Agnes," said Clarabelle.

Agnes looked. "Your toe is poking through your sneakers."

"That's right," said Clarabelle. "I need new shoes, and I want to get a pair just like yours!"

"I know the way to the store," Agnes said. "Come with me."

41

The store was big with lots to see. Agnes and Clarabelle wanted to try everything. They sprayed the perfumes. They tried on hats and scarves. They posed with the mannequins.

"This is the best day ever," said Clarabelle.

"Chicken shoes are on the third floor," said Agnes. She stepped toward the escalator.

"Wait, Agnes," Clarabelle said. "Will you promise me one thing?"

"What?" asked Agnes.

"Promise that you will not lose me."

"I promise," said Agnes.

"Cross your heart, hope to die?" asked Clarabelle.

"Stick a corncob in my eye," said Agnes. "I am your best friend. I will not lose you."

The escalator was crowded.

Clarabelle had to hop up and down to keep her eyes on Agnes's pink ears.

Her toe was still poking out of her sneaker. It felt itchy. She leaned down to scratch it.

When she stepped off the escalator, she took Agnes's hoof. "*Eeeee!*" Clarabelle ruffled her feathers.

She was not holding Agnes's hoof. She was holding a strange bear's paw.

"Little chicken," said the bear, "are you lost?"

Clarabelle could not answer. She could not speak at all.

She dropped the paw and began to spin around and around.

She did not see shoes. She did not see Agnes.

The bear was right.

She was lost.

No matter where she ran, she was in the wrong place. She ran to the bedding department and bounced high on the mattresses to find Agnes's head.

She ran to the bathroom and crouched down low to find Agnes's hooves.

She ran up and down every floor. She clucked around every corner.

She saw a security guard.

She saw a clerk at the register.

She saw moms and dads.

She saw other kids.

But she still did not see Agnes.

Agnes does not know where I am, thought Clarabelle.

Nobody knows where I am.

I am never, ever going to be found.

This is the worst day ever!

In a dressing room, Clarabelle sat in front of a three-way mirror. At least she could pretend there were three more chickens around her.

"Clarabelle Chicken!" called a voice from everywhere.

It was Agnes's voice. But it was very, very loud.

"Yes!" answered Clarabelle with all of her might.

Agnes was nowhere in sight, but Clarabelle heard her again.

"Clarabelle Chicken, please go to the information booth on the first floor!"

"Okay!" answered Clarabelle. "I will!"

Clarabelle ran out of the dressing room. She jumped back on the escalator and went down until it could not take her down any farther.

She knew she was on the first floor.

She sprinted to the information booth.

There was Agnes.

"I'm sorry I lost you," Agnes said.

"That's okay," panted Clarabelle.

"We're together now. But how did you make your voice so loud?"

"I used the loudspeaker. That way, I knew you would hear me. Are you ready to get your new shoes now?"

Clarabelle shook her head.

"I want to leave this store of lostness," she said. "The sneakers I have are just fine."

Agnes looked down at her friend's old sneakers and her sticking-out toe.

"You still need new ones," said Agnes. "But you can have mine."

"Really?"

"Sure. I have lots of other pairs. Let's go home."

And so they did.

Chapter 4
Winter: Perfect Pizza

"Do you smell that?" Agnes asked, with a twitch of her snout.

Clarabelle popped out from under a snowman's hat. "I don't smell anything from all the way up here!"

"It smells like someone's roasting chestnuts," said Agnes. "That means

it's time for me to make my famous Piggy Chestnut Pizza Pie."

"Yum!" Clarabelle clucked. "I'll help!"

"It starts with perfect chestnuts," Agnes said.

"I'm on it," said Clarabelle.

Together, Agnes and Clarabelle

went to Farmer Brown's orchard to
look for chestnuts.

Some were too warty. Some
were too lumpy. One looked like

Clarabelle's uncle Fred. One made Agnes scream.

"Good thing I've been doing my chicken chin-ups so I can carry this heavy bag," said Clarabelle.

Back at Agnes's house, they put the chestnuts in a pot to boil. Then they peeled them.

"What else can we put on your famous pizza pie?" wondered Clarabelle.

Agnes was already rummaging through the kitchen cupboards.

"Popcorn," she said. "And cheese. Lots and lots of cheese."

"And white chocolate chips," said Clarabelle. "Those go with everything."

They rolled the dough and popped the popcorn and grated the cheese.

"Whew, this is hard," said Clarabelle. "I'm really working up

an appetite." She pecked at a white chocolate chip.

"Don't eat that," Agnes said with a snort. "It's for the pizza."

Agnes patted down the crust into a perfect circle.

Clarabelle added the toppings and pinched the edges.

Together they carefully slid the pizza into the oven.

Soon the whole kitchen was filled with the smell of cheesy

chestnut-popcorn–white-chocolate pizza deliciousness.

PING! went the timer.

Slo-o-owly, Agnes and Clarabelle removed the piping-hot pizza pie from the oven and set it to cool on the windowsill.

Agnes pressed her hooves to her heart and sighed. "Oh! It's even more beautiful than I could have imagined."

Clarabelle hopped up onto the

stool. She held the pizza slicer high over her head. "INCOMING!"

"STOP!" bellowed Agnes.

"*Squawwk!*" Clarabelle fell back in surprise. "Agnes! What's wrong?!"

"Nothing is wrong," said Agnes. "In fact, it's perfect. The crust is browned."

"Just the way I like it!" said Clarabelle.

"The cheese and white chocolate melted to make a snowy lawn."

"They looked good unmelted too," said Clarabelle.

"The pieces of popcorn and chestnuts are like snowballs. This pizza looks like a winter wonderland."

"Yes," agreed Clarabelle. "And it also looks like a great big . . . pizza! Incoming!"

"Stop!" Agnes held up a hoof. "You know what I'm thinking, Clarabelle?"

"I sure do! You're thinking we can
eat this whole pizza in under ten
minutes!"

Agnes shook her head. "I'm

thinking this is pizza art. If you cut it up and pull it apart, you'll wreck it."

"But, Agnes," said Clarabelle, "I'm so peckish! My feathers are drooping! Didn't we make your famous Piggy Chestnut Pizza Pie so we could *eat* it?"

"But if we eat it," said Agnes, "then we don't get to look at it anymore."

Clarabelle put down the pizza slicer. She stared at her friend. She

stared back at the perfect chestnut
pizza pie.

Then she saw a box on the shelf.

"Agnes!" she said. "I have an idea!

Now that we made something beautiful to look at, let's make something quick to eat."

Agnes nodded. "That's a good idea, Clarabelle," she said. "I'm kind of hungry myself."

Adele Griffin is the author of a number of acclaimed series books for young readers, including the Witch Twins, Vampire Island, and most recently, the Oodlethunks: *Oona Finds an Egg* and *Steg-O-Normous*. She lives in Brooklyn, New York, with her family and their very small dog, Edith.

www.adelegriffin.com

Courtney Sheinmel has written over a dozen highly celebrated books for kids and teens, including the Stella Batts series for young readers; the YA novel *Edgewater*; and a new middle-grade series, the Kindness Club. She lives in New York City.

www.courtneysheinmel.com

Sara Palacios is the illustrator of the Pura Belpré Honor–winning picture book *Marisol McDonald Doesn't Match* by Monica Brown. She lives in San Francisco and Mexico City.

www.sarapalaciosillustrations.com